THE DREAM SHIP CRUISE

By

James T Gutka

From the Author

This is my first book, but I've been singing and creating stories for many years. This lullaby is a product of a dad and mom desperately struggling to find ways of getting their two daughters to calm down and sleep for the night. Hopefully, this soothing melody can help other parents do the same.

All Aboard,
The dream ship cruise

Bound for sleep,
and happiness too.

Sail Away,
Out to Sea

With just your dreams,
to guide you on your way.

The Gentle Waves,
Will Rock a bye

While the captain sings,
A lullaby

As we Sail,
On through the night

The stars will show us,
that everything will be alright.

Just Close your Eyes,
And Drift Away

Before too Long,
you'll be in another land

Full of all
Your Memories

And all the happiness,
that you could ever need

As we depart the
Dream ship cruise

With new memories,
Just waiting to be made

Ahoy,
Little Dreamer!

The story may be finished,
but the adventure has just begun!

You've sailed with the Dream Ship,
you've rocked with the gentle waves,
and you've drifted through the starry skies...

Now it's your turn to take the wheel!
Bring the pages to life with your own colors,
draw your own dream ship,
and let your imagination set sail.

Remember, every dreamer is also an artist,
and the sea of imagination has no end.

So grab your crayons, markers, or pencils,
and let's keep the adventure going,
one splash of color at a time!

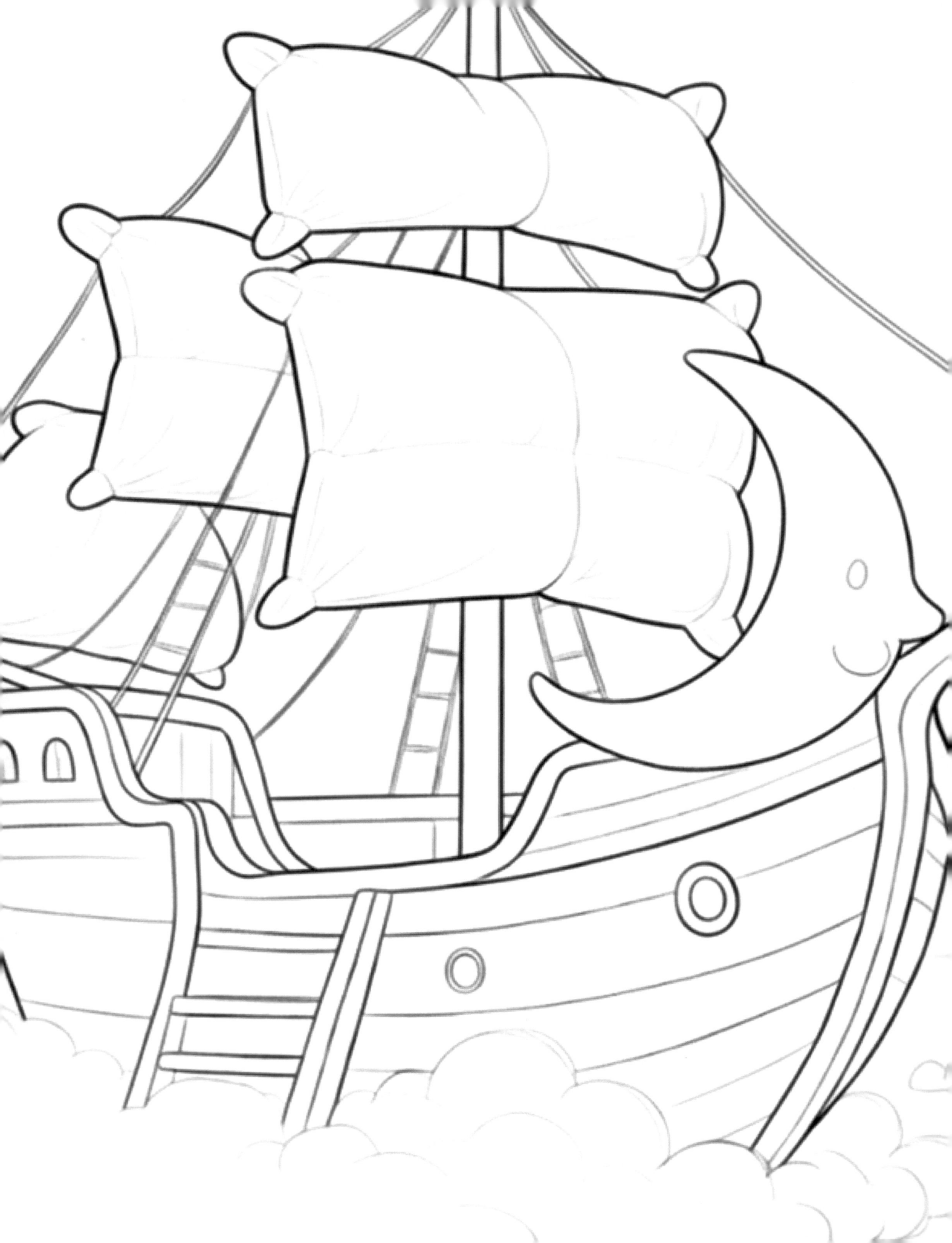

Connect
The Dot